WRITTEN & ILLUSTRATED BY CHRIS WORKMAN
IN COLLABORATION WITH KYLE LARSON

For the young race fans - never stop chasing your dreams.
And, for Abby, Asher & Jonah; you inspire me to keep chasing mine!

- Chris Workman

I have been around racing my whole life. As a kid, I went to tracks every weekend with my family to watch races, before I started racing karts myself when I was seven. I have always loved the sport, and am lucky enough to race cars for a living in NASCAR. I still love racing the same karts I drove as a kid, and I love encouraging other kids to get interested in racing; as a driver, crew member, or a fan.

Racing is a great sport where you can learn some great life lessons. I hope this book teaches you a little more about racing and if you don't already follow our sport, I hope you will after reading this book.

- Kyle Larson

FOREWORD

At only 25, Kyle Larson is already considered one of NASCAR's young superstar drivers, capable of collecting many trophies and earning multiple championships for years ahead on the sport's brightest stages. He has literally spent most of his life behind a steering wheel, racing and winning on all levels from midgets to sprint cars to stock cars. Larson brings an enthusiastic following and much promise to what should be a long and celebrated career in big-time auto racing.

His move up racing's ladder is a prime example to young fans and certainly aspiring racers, how far dedication and desire can take you. Set your sights high, work hard and never give up are lessons Kyle has learned along the way and still relies on today. They serve as solid reminders for his fans that anything is possible when you put both your heart and mind toward a goal.

- Holly Cain, NASCAR.com

ACKNOWLEDGEMENTS

Thanks to the many people within NASCAR, Kyle Larson Racing, Chip Ganassi Racing and General Motors who made it possible to create such an authentic children's book. "Kyle Loves Racing" is an officially licensed product of NASCAR, General Motors, LLC, Chip Ganassi Racing and Kyle Larson Racing.

"Kyle Larson" and the "Kyle Larson Racing" text logo are registered trademarks of Kyle Larson Racing and used with permission. "Chip Ganassi Racing" text and logo are registered trademarks of Chip Ganassi Racing Teams and used with permission.

Hi kids – I am race car driver Kyle Larson, and I love racing! I can't wait to share my story with you and show you what racing is all about! **ENJOY!**

ANYTHING, ANYWHERE, ANYTIME

I've raced since I was a young boy, and I've driven lots of different types of race cars. You'll see many of them in this book so I wanted to tell you a bit about them.

DIRT Cars: Midgets are small, basic dirt cars. Sprint cars are more powerful and faster. Some have a large metal wing on top to keep them on the ground!

FUN FACT: Unlike a car for the road, dirt cars only have one gear!

ENDURANCE SPORTS Car: These cars are built to last for races up to 24 hours. They have headlights to race at night and they race on road courses with left and right turns.

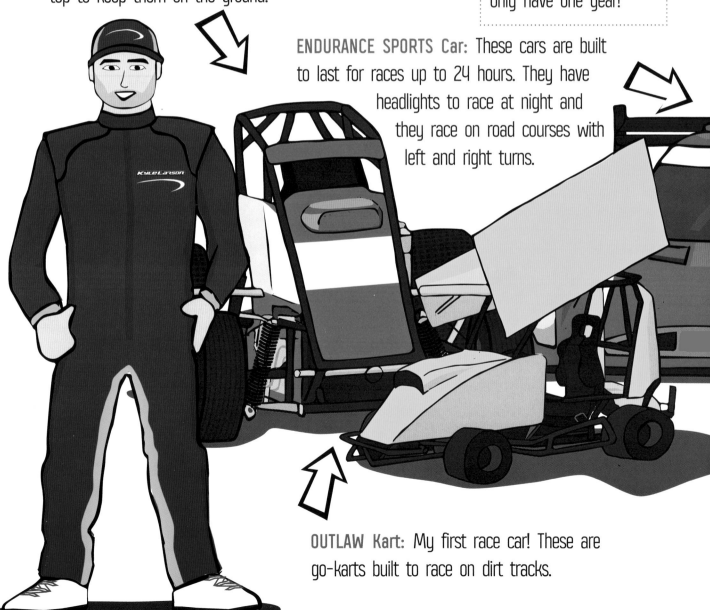

OUTLAW Kart: My first race car! These are go-karts built to race on dirt tracks.

FLAGS

If you watch just about any race, you'll see flags being waved at the drivers. These flags tell them things like "slow down and be careful" and "the race is over." Here are a few types of flags... and pay special attention to "restarts!"

Green: Waved when the race has started, or **restarted** after a caution. Go, go, go!

White: This flag is waved when there is only one lap left in the race!

Yellow (or caution): The cars need to slow down because it is raining, a car has spun or crashed, or something is lying on the track.

Checkered: This black & white flag is waved when the winner crosses the finish line. The race is over!

NASCAR STOCK Cars & Trucks: There are many different types of stock cars and trucks. The fastest are the Cup cars that I race for Chip Ganassi Racing.

FUN FACT: Each race season, I use several different paint schemes. But, my car is always number 42!

Kyle is sitting in his race car. He is excited because he is about to do his favorite thing in the world... **DRIVE AS FAST AS HE CAN!**

Kyle is **QUALIFYING** for a NASCAR Cup race. He is trying to set the fastest lap time possible.

Kyle swings his car out close to the wall to try and get a little **EXTRA SPEED.**

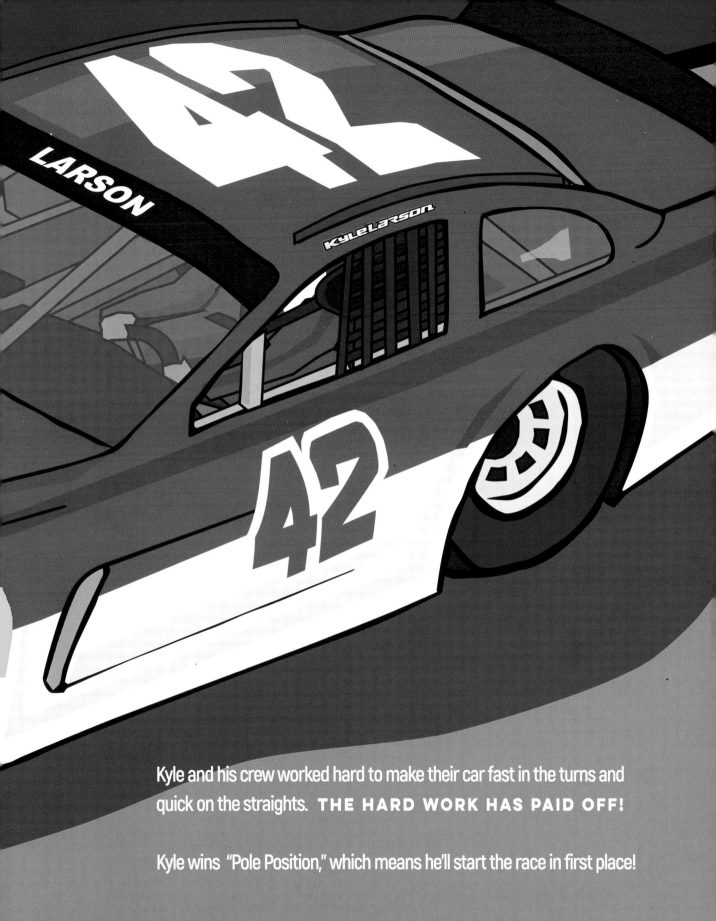

Kyle and his crew worked hard to make their car fast in the turns and quick on the straights. **THE HARD WORK HAS PAID OFF!**

Kyle wins "Pole Position," which means he'll start the race in first place!

Kyle and his crew chief talk about how to make his car **EVEN FASTER** for the race.

Then, Kyle sees some kids looking at his c[...]
One kid is wearing a dirt racing shirt, so K[...]
decides to talk to them.

KyleLarsc[...]

Kyle asks the kids if they like dirt track racing.

"Like it? **WE LOVE IT!**" the kids say. "We race go-karts on pavement. We want to try dirt racing since it looks like so much fun."

"Cool! Now that you are a NASCAR driver, why do you still race on dirt?" The kids ask.

"It's simple," says Kyle. "I will race **ANYTHING, ANYWHERE, ANYTIME!** Dirt tracks are like home to me."

"My parents took me to my first race when I was three weeks old. I grew up at the track watching, learning and racing," Kyle says.

"As I got older, I began racing sprint cars and midget cars at dirt tracks close to my hometown.

"Then, I started racing at tracks all across the country!"

"There is nothing like sliding a dirt car and **GOING THROUGH A TURN SIDEWAYS.**"

"One time, I won racing **THREE DIFFERENT TYPES OF CARS** in the same night at the 4-Crown Nationals!"

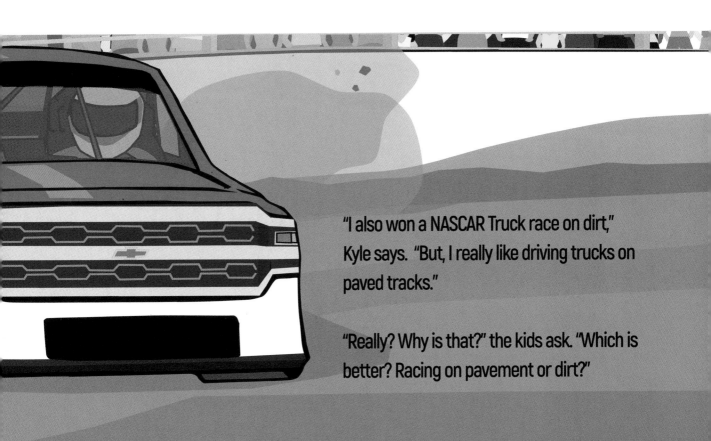

"I also won a NASCAR Truck race on dirt," Kyle says. "But, I really like driving trucks on paved tracks."

"Really? Why is that?" the kids ask. "Which is better? Racing on pavement or dirt?"

"THEY ARE BOTH GREAT," says Kyle, "because they are so different. The dirt track cars I race are nothing like stock cars in NASCAR."

WINGS

MORE POWER

ONE GEAR

GROOVED TIRES

OPEN-WHEELED

LIGHTER & SHORTER

"The fastest way to drive a dirt car is to **SLIDE IT SIDEWAYS** by keeping your foot on the gas pedal."

"You'll ruin your tires if you slide like that on pavement. So, you have to drive **MUCH SMOOTHER.** Paved tracks are also faster!"

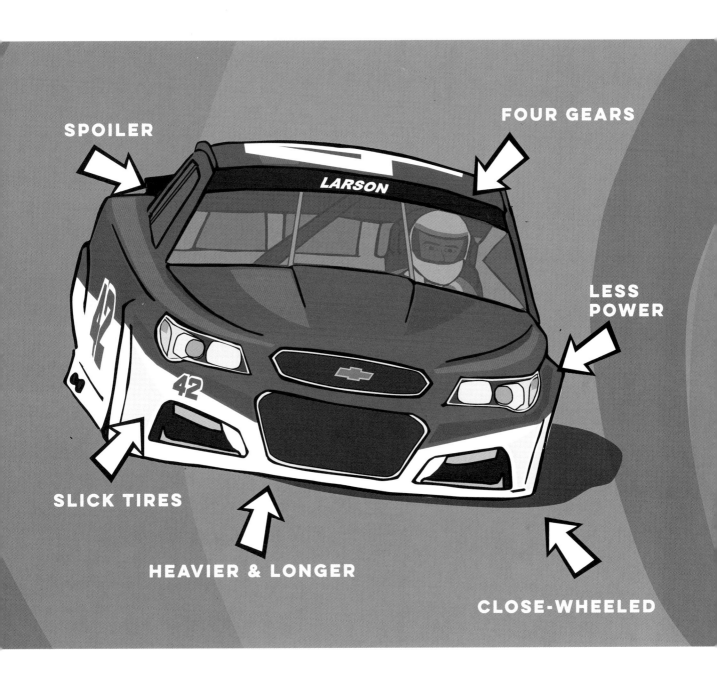

"There are more types of paved tracks to learn too, like small ovals, superspeedways and road courses."

"That's great!" Then the kids ask, "Do you have any other advice for young racers like us?

Kyle tells the kids to **NEVER GIVE UP.**

"I had a lot of spins, crashes and bad finishes my first few seasons in the NASCAR Cup Series. I knew I had to stay positive, learn from my mistakes, and remind myself that I race because I love it. **WINNING ISN'T EVERYTHING!**"

Kyle tells the kids that his patience finally paid off in his 99th NASCAR Cup race.

"We were at Michigan, which is a **REALLY FAST TRACK.** My car was great and I was able to stay near the front most of the race."

"There were several caution periods at the end of the race. I had to **NAIL MY RESTARTS** if I was going to win," Kyle said.

"**I SPUN MY TIRES** when the green flag dropped," said Kyle. "I thought I would get passed, but the guy next to me spun his tires too."

Then, I got **PUSHED FROM BEHIND** into the lead!"

"I stayed in the lead and crossed the finish line first," said Kyle.

"**I COULDN'T BELIEVE I HAD FINALLY WON!** I had fun doing burnouts after the race."

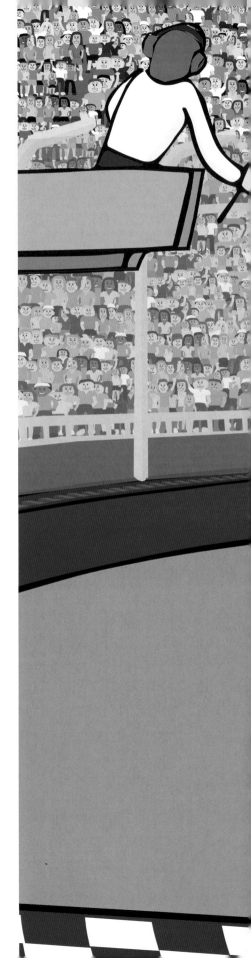

The kids ask Kyle if he thinks he can win his NASCAR Cup race this weekend.

Kyle smiles and says, "We'll see. First, I have my XFINITY race. If that goes well, I'll feel better about the Cup race."

Then, Kyle tells the kids he needs to go talk to his team. He says that he hopes the kids can come to his dirt race later that week.

The next day, **KYLE WINS HIS XFINITY RACE.**
He is excited for the big NASCAR Cup race the following day!

IT'S TIME FOR THE BIG RACE! Kyle signs autographs and talks to his guests. Then, it is time to sing "The Star-Spangled Banner" with his family.

Meanwhile, the kids and their parents get settled in their seats in the grandstands.

The announcer says, "Drivers, start your engines!" Kyle's engine comes to life with a **LOUD ROAARRR!!!**

Kyle and the other drivers follow the pace car for a few warmup laps to make sure the cars and track are safe for the race.

The green flag waves and the cars **SCREAM BY** to start the race.
The kids cheer for Kyle as he takes the lead!

Kyle's car is quick and he is able to stay in front of the other drivers.

BUT, THE RACE IS LONG. Kyle knows he needs to drive smart and fast if he is going to win the race.

ALL THE DRIVERS ARE RACING HARD.
Two cars bump into each other and one spins out. The yellow flag waves to slow the cars down for a caution period.

KYLE DIVES INTO THE PITS. His pit crew changes tires and fills up his tank.

HIS PIT CREW IS FAST, but a few other teams are faster. Kyle loses four positions and drops to fifth place.

KYLE WORKS HIS WAY THROUGH THE FIELD.

Before long, he is up to second place! Kyle drives as fast as he can to catch the leader.

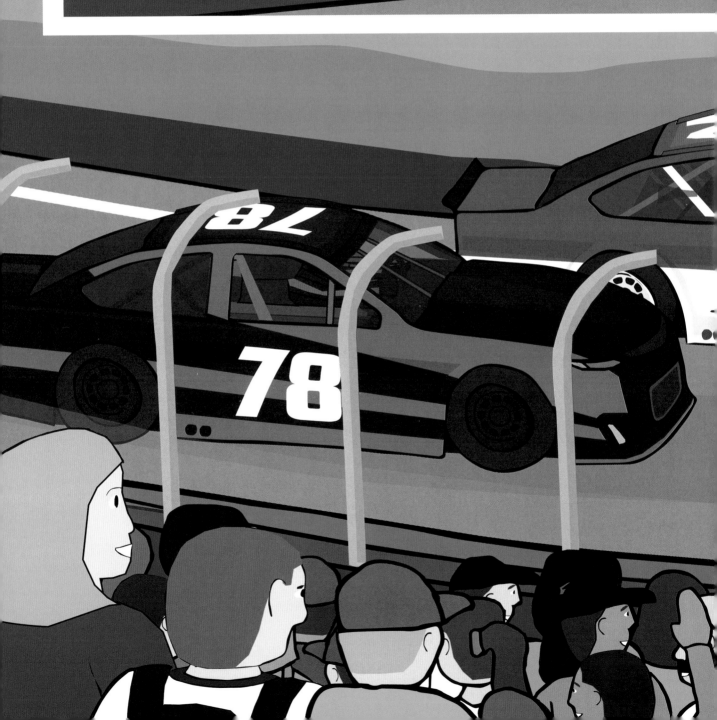

The kids watch as Kyle passes a car on the inside to take first place. They are on their feet CHEERING FOR THEIR HERO!

Kyle stays in the lead for much of the race. But, with about 50 laps to go, he needs to make a pit stop.

Kyle drops back to fourth place after the pit stop.

BUT, KYLE IS DETERMINED TO GET BACK INTO THE LEAD!

He moves inside the third-place car and races to to catch up to second place.

A few laps later, Kyle is back in the lead. **HE HAS TO KEEP PUSHING** because he has a car right on his tail! ⇨

With less than ten laps to go, Kyle comes into the pits for fresh tires. Three drivers decide not to pit and stay on track, which moves Kyle back to fourth place.

There aren't many laps left in the race so the drivers are racing hard to get ahead of their rivals. One of them crashes causing a caution period.

THE KIDS ARE NERVOUS FOR THE FINISH.

Can Kyle pass three cars with only seven laps to go to win the race?

KYLE'S CAR IS MUCH FASTER ON NEW TIRES.

He makes some great passes on the backstretch and moves into the lead.
There are only a few laps to go in the race!

Suddenly, a yellow flag waves after another car crashes.

Kyle is in first place, but he needs a **PERFECT RESTART** if he is going to win!

The kids are on the edges of their seats as the green flag waves!

As the drivers jump on the gas, Kyle spins his tires and slips into second.

KYLE IS DETERMINED TO GET BY FOR THE WIN!

He catches up to his rival and moves to the outside to make a tough pass in the first turn. He pulls ahead and stays in the lead the last few laps of the race!

The kids scream with excitement as Kyle crosses the finish line.

KYLE HAS WON THE RACE!

Kyle does a burnout in front of the crowd and heads to Victory Lane to

CELEBRATE HIS WIN!

BUT, THE FUN ISN'T OVER FOR KYLE!

In a few days, he has a dirt track race near his hometown. Can he win and make it three races in a row?

Kyle has a **BIG SMILE** under his helmet as he climbs into a sprint car. It feels great to be back at home and he can't wait to slide on the dirt!

As the green flag drops, Kyle enjoys the thrill of driving his sprint car quickly on a short track against lots of other drivers.

Kyle doesn't have a great race and finishes behind many of the other drivers, but that's OK.

HE LOVES RACING, and he is happy for the driver who won the race!

After the race, Kyle sees the kids. They tell Kyle they're sorry he lost.

Kyle says, "it's okay, **WINNING ISN'T EVERYTHING.** I had a blast!"

He gives the kids his racing gloves to remind them to work hard, chase their dreams and have fun racing... even if they don't always win!

THE STORY OF THE LADYBUG

You may have noticed a tiny ladybug sticker on my car right above my name. Did you wonder why it is there?

Ladybugs are a sign of good luck, but there is more to the story than that. Way back in 1980, a famous driver named Johnny Rutherford had a ladybug land on his racing glove right before the start of the Indy 500... and he won the race!

My mom and dad have always been huge racing fans and loved watching Johnny win that race.

When I started racing, my mom put ladybug stickers on my cars and she has been doing it ever since for a bit of added good luck!

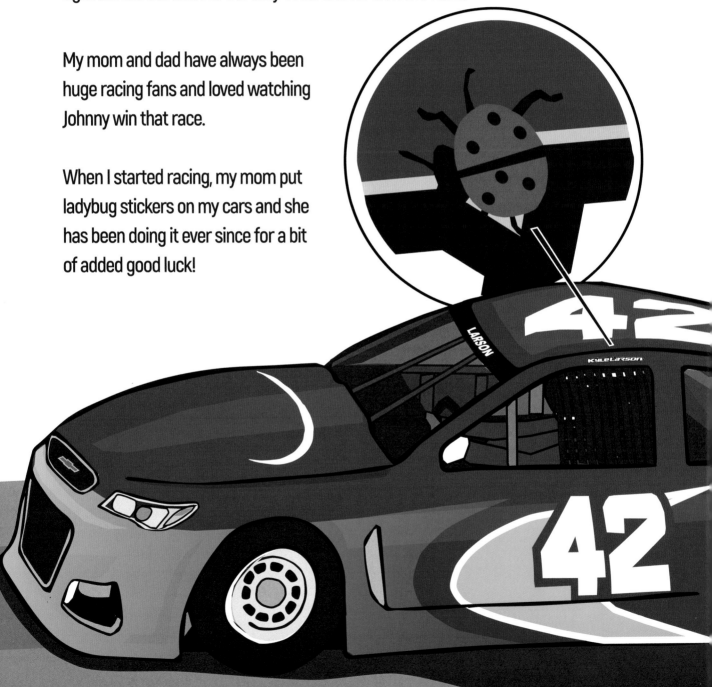

WANT TO BECOME A RACE CAR DRIVER?

If sliding a car on dirt or flying down the back straight of an oval track at 200 mph is your dream, that is awesome! Being a race car driver is great, but it takes some hard work. Here are some things you can do while you are young to get ready.

TRY KARTING OR GO TO A RACE

Give racing a try with some karting to see if you really like it. Or, go to a local race and see what the drivers, crew chiefs and pit crews do and see if you want to do it too!

EAT RIGHT & EXERCISE

You have to be in great shape to drive a race car! Be sure to eat right and stay active so you have energy to drive a race car for several hours and stay focused.

STUDY HARD

While racing requires a great deal of physical activity, it also requires quick thinking on and off the track. Learning math and science will help you work with your crew chief to make the race car faster. And, being a good writer and speaker are important for working with your team, sponsors and the news media.

STAY POSITIVE

Becoming a NASCAR driver isn't easy, but you can do it. Listen to advice, believe in yourself and try your best!

Thanks for reading! Have fun and I will see you at the track!

If you enjoyed this book and want to share more stories about racing with your kids, go to ApexLegends.com to learn more about our other titles and exclusive products like racing coloring books.

JOSEF, THE INDY CAR DRIVER

"When it comes to fast reads, 'Josef, the Indy Car Driver' deserves a spot on any young racing fan's podium--or bookshelf." - AutoWeek

Apex Legends and Verizon IndyCar Series star Josef Newgarden teamed up to create a unique racing-themed children's picture book unlike any other. "Josef, The Indy Car Driver" mixes Indy car racing education with entertaining on-track action that is sure to please budding race fans and their parents!

THE SPECTACLE - CELEBRATING THE HISTORY OF THE INDIANAPOLIS 500

"For young students and race fans who are taking an interest in the history of the Indianapolis 500 and would like to learn more, this book will answer A LOT of their questions." -Donald Davidson, Historian, Indianapolis Motor Speedway

"The Spectacle - Celebrating the History of the Indianapolis 500" is a mix of historical fact and entertainment for young readers and race fans to learn about The Greatest Spectacle in Racing - the Indianapolis 500.

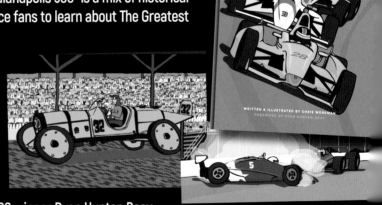

The book features a vast number of drivers, teams and race cars that have made an impact in the rich history of racing at the Brickyard. The book breaks the content into a series of short topical sections such as The Golden Era, The British Invasion and The Four-Timer Club.

A. Foyt makes a cameo; Foreword by 2014 Indy 500 winner Ryan Hunter-Reay.

MORE GREAT BOOKS ON THE WAY!

Apex Legends is working on a Le Mans book featuring the Ford GT, plus several other projects are taking shape. Sign up The Inside Line enewsletter at ApexLegends.com to get a code for 10% a future purchase. Or, follow Apex Legend's social media for new product updates, special offers and more!